SHADOW·PLAY

SHADOW·PLAY

STORY BY **PAUL FLEISCHMAN**

PICTURES BY **ERIC BEDDOWS**

A CHARLOTTE ZOLOTOW BOOK
Harper & Row, Publishers

Library of Congress Cataloging-in-Publication Data
Fleischman, Paul.
    Shadow play / by Paul Fleischman ; illustrations by Eric Beddows.
        p.   cm.
    "A Charlotte Zolotow book."
    Summary: While visiting the country fair, a brother and sister are
enthralled by a shadow puppet show presentation of "Beauty and the
Beast" in which all the shadows are made by one man.
    ISBN 0-06-021858-4. — ISBN 0-06-021865-7 (lib. bdg.)
    [1. Shadow pantomimes and plays—Fiction.   2. Fairy tales.]
I. Beddows, Eric, 1951–   ill.   II. Title.
PZ7.F59918Sh   1990   89-26874
[E]—dc20   CIP
                                                              AC

For Zachary

"Come on. We've only got twenty
cents left."

"Kings and queens! Maybe he'll give
us his autograph."

"Once, long ago, there lived a rich merchant with six sons and six daughters and three servants for each. One day a messenger brought him dire news: All his ships had been sunk by a storm. He and his family were ruined. They moved far from the sea, to a tiny cottage. The children had no choice but to plow and sow and spin, complaining all the while— except for the youngest daughter, called Beauty."

"Soon after, the merchant heard that one of his ships, filled with spices, had survived. He prepared to ride to the coast to meet it. Sure that they were rich again, his children asked him to buy them fine clothes and dazzling jewels. Beauty, however, asked only for a rose."

"The merchant reached the sea, but found his ship empty. Sadly, he set off for home, and lost his way in the woods. Night came on. Snow began to fall. Through the veil of flakes he spotted a castle, and was amazed to find that no snow had fallen on the path leading up to it."

"He knocked. When no one answered, he stepped inside and beheld a sumptuous dinner waiting on a table. Hungrily, he ate it, then fell asleep on a bed nearby."

13

"In the morning he found tarts, cider, and oranges waiting on the table. Astonished, the merchant ate and prepared to go on his way. How sad his children would be, he thought, to find he'd not brought them the presents they'd asked for. Leaving the castle, he noticed a rose, recalled Beauty's request, and picked it."

"Then the merchant turned and saw a frightful beast."

"STUPENDO!"

"Absolutely amazing!"

"Amazing, that is, that we of all people should forget the moral of the play. For in just such a fashion, through love, Beauty caused the Beast to be changed into the handsome prince he actually was. Teaching us that appearances are as thin and deceptive—as shadows."

"Who would care to step backstage
and behold the truth of our tale?"

"It's you!"

The End

6